Dinner at Magritte's

MICHAEL GARLAND

DUTTON CHILDREN'S BOOKS NEW YORK

Notes about surrealism and brief biographies of the
three artists—Magritte, Dalí, and Garland—
can be found on the last page of the book.

The illustrations were painted in oils and
reproduced in full color.

Library of Congress Cataloging-in-Publication Data
Garland, Michael, date
Dinner at Magritte's / by Michael Garland.—1st ed.
p. cm.
Summary: Young Pierre spends the day with
surrealist artists René Magritte and Salvador Dalí.
ISBN 0-525-45336-9
1. Magritte, René, 1898–1967—Juvenile fiction.
2. Dalí, Salvador, 1904–1989—Juvenile fiction. [1. Magritte, René,
1898–1967—Fiction. 2. Dalí, Salvador, 1904–1989—Fiction.
3. Artists—Fiction. 4. France—Fiction.] I. Title.
PZ7.G18413Di 1995   [Fic]—dc20
94-28257 CIP AC

Published in the United States 1995 by Dutton Children's Books,
a division of Penguin Books USA Inc.
375 Hudson Street, New York, New York 10014

Editor: Riki Levinson

Printed in Hong Kong   First Edition
10 9 8 7 6 5 4 3 2 1

for my wife, Peggy

Paris was too hot and noisy in the summertime. So on the weekends, Pierre and his parents went to their cottage in the country.

There it was cool and quiet. A little too quiet, Pierre thought. Nothing to do, and no children to play with. His parents sat as still as stone while Pierre tried to imagine something interesting to do to fill his boring day.

Across the lawn was René and Georgette Magritte's house. René was an artist. Pierre's father said they were strange people, but Pierre liked them a lot. Sometimes he could hear music and laughter coming from their house.

"I think I'll go next door," Pierre announced, "and visit the Magrittes."

"That's nice, Pierre," said his parents quietly.

Pierre hurried to the Magrittes' house.

Magritte opened the door. "*Bonjour,* Pierre. Come in!" said Magritte. "Georgette, it's our young friend, Pierre."

"Welcome, Pierre," said Georgette warmly. "You've picked a good day for a visit. Our friend is coming to dinner. I'm sure you'll like him. I hope you can stay."

"Oh yes!" said Pierre happily.

Before the guest arrived, Pierre watched Magritte work in his studio. Pierre was puzzled because Magritte was looking at an egg on the table but was painting something entirely different.

"I don't see any bird," Pierre said. "There's only an egg!"

"Anyone can try to paint what they see," Magritte replied. "I like to paint what I think. I paint what I dream. So, when people look at my paintings, they can see what's in my mind. Can you?"

"Oh yes," said Pierre. "I mean, I think so."

After a while, there was a knock on the studio door. Magritte opened it. A tall thin man, his cape swirling about him, strode into the room. With a dramatic gesture, he took off his wide-brimmed hat and threw back his head.

"You're five minutes late!" Magritte said to the man. "Did you dilly, Dalí?"

"You never tire of that old joke, do you, Magritte?" the man said, smiling broadly at his host. "And who is this?" he asked, looking at Pierre.

"He's our neighbor, Pierre," replied Magritte. "Pierre, this is our good friend, Salvador Dalí. He's an artist too."

Pierre smiled at the peculiar-looking man, but he wasn't quite sure what to make of him.

Georgette suggested a walk before dinner. So they
all strolled among the trees behind Magritte's house.

Pierre had seen these woods before, but he wondered
why they looked so unusual today.

When their walk was over, the happy group decided to play croquet. It was a little tricky for Pierre to whack his ball through the wickets, but he did it, at last!

Before they could finish their game, it started to rain cats and dogs. They all dashed for the house. No one minded because they were very hungry by now.

Dinner was served on the big table in the cozy kitchen. Georgette's centerpiece was an old boot overflowing with lilies and hollyhock. Everyone was talking and laughing at the same time.

"I've made my two favorite recipes!" announced
Georgette proudly. "Flying Fish Soup and Partridge Pie!"
"*Magnifique!*" Dalí exclaimed.

Pierre was too surprised to speak.

After dinner they played charades, but Pierre was
tired.

"It's getting late," said Dalí, looking at the clock.
"I don't want to miss my train."

Dalí hugged everyone. "Well, *mes amis, au revoir*," he said, sweeping out the door with a flourish.

Pierre thanked the Magrittes. He'd had a wonderful time. "I really enjoyed myself."

"We did too," they replied. "Come again soon."

When Pierre got home, his mother and father were in the parlor, the same as ever, as still as stone.

Pierre was too tired to talk, so he just said, "Good night."

"Good night, Pierre," replied his parents quietly.

Upstairs, Pierre settled into his bed. He closed his eyes and thought about his visit and Magritte's painting. Soon dream clouds filled his room. As Pierre drifted deeper into the night sky, he wondered what he would do and see tomorrow. Would it be a day as special as this one?

René Magritte and Salvador Dalí, who became friends during the 1920s, were surrealist artists.

Surrealist paintings, often called Magic Realism, combine elements that usually don't belong together. This odd mixture of components can achieve the effect of strange, sometimes extraordinary, imagery. The paintings may seem mysterious, as Magritte's do, or even nightmarish, like Dalí's.

In this book, Michael Garland's pictures include many surreal images. Why don't you look at them again and *see* how many you can find?

MAGRITTE, René François-Ghislain, 1898–1967, was born in Lessines, Belgium. His paintings have an eerie, dreamlike quality. Though he painted in a very realistic way, it was the objects that he chose to combine, and how he used his incredible imagination, that made his work so different.

René Magritte was a very reserved person. Despite the fame that his work brought to him, he and his wife, Georgette, lived a private, middle-class life.

DALI, Salvador Felipe Jacinto, 1904–1989, was born in Figueras, Spain. Art reviewers described his work as wild distortions of reality. Dalí called his surrealistic paintings "hand-painted dream photographs." In addition to painting, he did lithographs, designed theater sets and jewelry, and was a sculptor and writer.

Dalí, in real life, was flamboyant. He was as colorful as his paintings.

GARLAND, Michael Patrick, who was born in 1952 in New York City, studied at Pratt Institute in Brooklyn, New York. His varied artwork ranges from fine art to magazine covers, advertisements, and book illustration. Garland's paintings have garnered many awards, including the Society of Illustrators Silver Medal in 1994.

This is his third picture book as both author and illustrator.